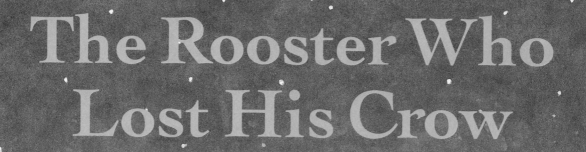

The Rooster Who Lost His Crow

Wendy Cheyette Lewison

PICTURES BY *Thor Wickstrom*

Dial Books for Young Readers
New York

Published by Dial Books for Young Readers
A Division of Penguin Books USA Inc.
375 Hudson Street
New York, New York 10014

Designed by Nancy R. Leo
Printed in Hong Kong
First Edition
1 3 5 7 9 10 8 6 4 2

Library of Congress Cataloging in Publication Data
Lewison, Wendy Cheyette.
The rooster who lost his crow / by Wendy Cheyette Lewison ;
pictures by Thor Wickstrom.—1st ed.
p.   cm.
Summary: After a bee scares the cock-a-doodle-doo out of him,
Rooster anxiously searches the entire barnyard for it.
ISBN 0-8037-1545-5 (trade). — ISBN 0-8037-1546-3 (library)
[1. Roosters—Fiction. 2. Domestic animals—Fiction.]
I. Wickstrom, Thor, ill.   II. Title.
PZ7.L5884Ro 1995   [E]—dc20   93-28059   CIP   AC

The full-color artwork for this book was prepared using pen and ink,
watercolor and gouache. It was then scanner-separated and reproduced as
red, blue, yellow, and black halftones.

*For John, Beth, and David—my rooster
and two little chickens*

W.C.L.

For Sosha

T.W.

EVERY MORNING, just as night was giving way to day, just as the orange sun was peeking over the chicken coop, Rooster hurried out into the farmyard.

Quickly he ran, past the hens in the henhouse clucking, past the pigs in the pigsty oinking, past the cows in the barn mooing, and past the farmer in the farmhouse sleeping.

When he reached the old wooden fence, he flew up
to the highest post where he settled his feathers, took a
deep breath, threw back his head, and crowed, "COCK-
A-DOODLE-DOO!"

The farmer opened one eye.

"COCK-A-DOODLE-DOO!" crowed Rooster again.

The farmer opened the other eye. "Guess it's time to wake up," he said.

He dressed in his overalls and pulled on his boots. Then out he went to gather the eggs, feed the pigs, and milk the cows. And all was right with the world.

Until one morning, when Rooster flew to his post.
He settled his feathers, took a deep breath, threw back
his head, and started to crow. Suddenly a tiny bee flew
right up in front of Rooster's open beak—BUZZ-Z-Z!—
scaring the cock-a-doodle-doo right out of him.

"I'll try again," said Rooster.

So he settled his feathers more carefully, took a deeper breath, threw his head back farther, and tried again. But nothing came out, no sound at all. Not even a little tiny peep-peep-peep.

The hens clucked, "Where is the farmer to gather our eggs?" The pigs oinked, "Where is the farmer to give us our breakfast?" The cows mooed, "Where is the farmer to milk us?" And Rooster cried, "Where is my cock-a-doodle-doo?"

"Maybe it's stuck down there," clucked the hens, pointing to Rooster's throat. So Rooster opened his mouth wide and all the hens looked down his throat. But no cock-a-doodle-doo was there.

"Maybe it's somewhere in the grass," oinked the pigs.
So Rooster pecked around in the grass with his beak,
and the pigs sniffed around in the grass with their
snouts. But no cock-a-doodle-doo was in the grass.

"Maybe it went home," mooed the cows. So Rooster ran all the way home. But no cock-a-doodle-doo was there.

"It's gone! I've lost it!" cried Rooster. "I must find my cock-a-doodle-doo, or the farmer won't know that it's time to wake up!"

So Rooster searched all over the farm.

He looked in the shed. A tractor was in the shed. But no cock-a-doodle-doo.

He looked in the pond. Some ducks were swimming in the pond. But no cock-a-doodle-doo.

He looked behind a haystack. A pitchfork was behind the haystack. But no cock-a-doodle-doo.

He looked in the cornfield. A mouse was hiding in
the cornfield. But no cock-a-doodle-doo.

He looked and looked. But his cock-a-doodle-doo did not seem to be anywhere. Rooster did not know what else to do. So he stood on a rusty milk bucket, looking sad.

Suddenly Rooster heard a great peeping and squawking. It was coming from the chicken coop. What could be the matter?

Rooster stopped thinking about his cock-a-doodle-doo. He ran over and peeked in the chicken coop window.

In one corner of the coop the tiny yellow chicks were all huddled together. In another corner, sneaking closer and closer to them, was a big old fox!

In an instant Rooster flew into the coop. He planted himself right down between the frightened chicks and the old fox.

Then he fluffed up his feathers so that he looked big
and mean, took a deep breath, and threw back his head.

"COCK-A-DOODLE-DOO!" crowed Rooster.

It was the loudest cock-a-doodle-doo Rooster had ever crowed. It was also the loudest cock-a-doodle-doo the fox had ever heard, and he didn't wait around for the farmer to come running, but skedaddled out of that chicken coop as fast as he could go.

"I found it!" crowed Rooster. "My cock-a-doodle-doo was right here in the chicken coop!" Everyone agreed that the bee had indeed scared the cock-a-doodle-doo into the chicken coop.

As for the farmer, when he heard that very loud cock-a-doodle-doo, he opened both eyes at once. "Guess it's time to wake up," he said.

He dressed in his overalls and pulled on his boots. Then out he went to gather the eggs, feed the pigs, and milk the cows.

And all was right with the world.